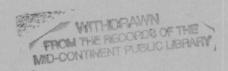

The Snowman in the Moon

Written and Illustrated by
Stephen Heigh

Edited by
Kevin Burton

KRBY Creations, LLC
Bay Head, New Jersey

ISBN-10   0-9745715-5-5
ISBN-13   987-0-9745715-5-3
Library of Congress Control Number: 2005902251

Printed and Bound in China

Graphic Design and Production:
Judy Cardella Graphic Design
New Egypt, NJ

Editor and Publisher:
Kevin R. Burton
KRBY Creations, LLC
Post Office Box 327, Bay Head, NJ 08742
www.KRBYCreations.com

Dedicated to
Dorothy and Thomas with Love
for believing in me.

Visit

www.SnowmanintheMoon.com

for updates, free coloring pages, and other fun items.

There's a little bit of Woodstream County in all of us. A town with friends and neighbors, children playing, and where everyone dreams. Woodstream County had not seen a good snowfall for a long, long time. The children had forgotten all about sledding or building snowmen. But one December day, something magical happened.

It was a crisp winter day and the children were playing together, building forts and running through the woods. They were having a lot of fun, but they knew it would soon be time to head home for dinner and bed.

On their way home, two of the children looked up in the sky and noticed that the clouds were shaped like snow-covered hills, with pine trees and even what looked like a snowman. The town had wished for a big snow so many times before, but it never came. Tonight seemed no different. There was no snow in the forecast.

That night the two children were lying on the ground, looking at the moon and stars in the night sky. The sky was a deep blue and the air was very still and quiet. The moon seemed unusually bright this night, and at exactly the same time the two children said, "I wish it would snow." And at just that moment the face of a snowman appeared in the moon — and then quickly disappeared.

They rubbed their eyes and one of them said, "Did you see that?" "Yes I did! It's a sign! It's a sign! We're going to have a big snow tonight!" The children scrambled to their feet, full of excitement and anticipation. The sky turned misty and a gentle, magical breeze filled the air. It swept all across Woodstream County.

The two children went from house to house telling everyone about the snowman in the moon and the magic in the air. "It's going to snow tonight! We saw a snowman in the moon!" But their friends and neighbors all said "It hasn't snowed here in years. You're dreaming."

Some townspeople turned on the television to watch the late news. They too longed for it to snow. But the weatherman had no reports on any snow. "The Snowman in the Moon," the neighbors thought, "Childhood dreams." Deep down in their hearts, however, the townspeople all really wanted to believe. Many added a quick wish to their evening prayers that the children's dreams would come true tonight.

The children did believe it would snow. They knew that the snowman in the moon was real. And as the children slept, they dreamed of playing in the snow with their family and friends. It was fantastic, and everyone was happy. They built an amazing snowman together. It stood almost twenty feet tall – a classic snowman everyone would remember.

The air grew misty outside
as the children dreamed.
Their bedroom windows
became foggy and were
soon covered with frost.
There was magic in the air.
The Snowman in the Moon
appeared through the trees
as the town slept under the
night sky.

The snowman in the moon had work to do and got to it. The clouds rolled through Woodstream County, bringing gentle waves of falling snow. The snow sparkled like diamonds as the moonlight illuminated its path. Woodstream County would have a very special treat tonight.

The next morning when the children awoke, they went to their frosted windows and wiped them clean to see outside. They jumped with joy at what they saw. It had snowed all night! This was not just any snowfall. It was the largest snowfall in the history of Woodstream County.

There was a knock at the front door. When they opened the door they saw everyone from their town smiling and excited. They said "Well come on! We've got a snowman to build. Your Snowman in the Moon was right after all!"

So all of Woodstream County came together and built the most amazing snowman. It was just like the snowman the children had dreamed about the night before. When they were done, everyone gathered around their amazing sculpture of snow. They were proud of what they had built together. Young and old were enjoying the day's events.

The moon was full and bright, and the sky was clear. They all looked up at the moon and said "Thank you, Snowman in the Moon." A hush came over the crowd, and to their amazement the Snowman in the Moon appeared to all of them. He was smiling and shined brightly on their creation. It was a magical and special night.

The End

If you believe, all things are possible.
Together, young and old, rich and poor,
believing in our hearts can make reality from things hoped for,
and can make the unseen come true.